Don't be afraid of t

Table of contents

Chapter 1: Lock in

Chapter 2: The Man in the white Hat

Chapter 3: The Doctor's House

Chapter 4: The Last Chance

Chapter 5: Mother and Daughter

Chapter 6: Deepened

Chapter 7: The Talk Between Worlds

Chapter 8: The Descent

Chapter 9: The Cabin

Chapter 10: Poisoned Love

Chapter 11: The Tree of Light

Chapter 12: The Choice

Chapter 13: Tree Calling

Chapter 14: Time of Moon and Star

Chapter 1: Lock In

The room was silent for a moment, but the silence was thick with anticipation. Seven strangers, trapped in an unfamiliar room with no windows and no doors. The walls, pale and peeling, gave no hints about where they were. In the middle of the room, a dim light hung, flickering now and then, as though struggling to stay alive.

Four women: Mary, Brittany, Alisa, and Lauryn.

Three men: Noah, Joseph, and William.

They started with simple questions, each of them cautious, feeling the others out. Mary was the first to speak, her voice steady but with an edge of wariness. “Does anyone know how we got here?” she asked, glancing around.

No one answered, but the question lingered, pushing them to offer whatever small fragments of truth they could remember.

One by one, they began to tell their stories. At first, they were polite, restrained. Brittany recounted snippets of her life—a few career highlights, a few relationships left in the past. Joseph, sitting opposite her, mentioned his last memory was simply being at home before everything went dark.

As each spoke, the others grew quieter, listening more intently as the stories took darker turns. With each revelation, the mood in the room thickened. Secrets began to surface, slipping out like whispers each couldn't quite control.

Alisa admitted to having been estranged from her family, her voice cracking as she spoke. William shifted uncomfortably as he mentioned an old mistake that still haunted him. Lauryn, her gaze distant, recounted a memory that seemed to fill the room with an almost tangible sorrow.

Noah and Joseph both shared glimpses of regrets, each story casting them in a new, unsettling light. In those moments, as they revealed the darkness they carried, it was as if the walls closed in a bit more, each secret binding them together yet pushing them further apart.

They began to see each other differently. Trust faded into curiosity laced with suspicion, each wondering what the others were hiding.

Chapter 2: The Man in the White Hat

The room was swallowed by darkness. Just as quickly, the darkness lifted, and the seven people found themselves in a new setting—a grand, dimly lit bar-restaurant. Soft jazz music played in the background, and the air smelled faintly of oak and leather. They looked around, bewildered, taking in the polished tables, the ornate bar lined with bottles, and the quiet elegance of their surroundings.

At the center of the room stood a man in a pristine white suit and hat, his expression both calm and foreboding. His eyes were shadowed under the brim, but his gaze held each of them, his presence commanding absolute silence. He looked like someone out of another time, or perhaps from a dream—or a nightmare.

“Welcome,” the man said smoothly, his voice rich and steady. “I am your last chance. You may call me the Man in the White Hat. You’ve each been brought here to confront what you cannot escape: the truths of your lives, the moments where you each… failed.”

The room was quiet, the tension thick as the strangers glanced at each other uneasily.

The Man in the White Hat gestured for them to speak, and slowly, one by one, they began to share their stories.

Alisa spoke first, her voice rough. "I came from a rough home, abusive parents… but I always told myself I'd rise above it. Only, I didn't. I treated people just like they treated me, pushing them away, hurting them because it's all I knew."

Mary cleared her throat, the shame visible in her eyes. "I was a junkie," she confessed, her voice quiet but resolute. "Needles, pills—whatever I could find. It almost destroyed me. I ruined every good thing in my life. It's a dark road, one I'm still struggling to leave behind."

Brittany spoke next, her tone tinged with regret. "I was furious with my parents. They never let me be who I wanted to be. One night, I put a pill in each of their drinks, just to shut them up, I guess. They didn't die, but… they've been sick ever since. Years have passed, and I'm the reason they suffer."

Lauryn sat silently for a moment before speaking. "I come from a place where fighting was normal. One day, I fought with my cousin, my best friend. It was just supposed to be another fight, but I lost control." Her voice cracked. "She's brain-dead now. I did time for it, but I live with her face in my mind every single day."

Noah, who had been staring at the floor, finally lifted his head. "I was a doctor, always working long hours, so focused I didn't pay attention to anything else. One night, I left something on the stove and passed out from exhaustion." He took a breath, his voice shaking. "The house burned down… with my family inside. I was the only one they pulled out. The guilt… it never leaves."

Joseph's face twisted as he spoke, his words tinged with bitterness. "My wife and I… we had a terrible fight. I pushed her, just a shove. She fell down the stairs and ended up in a wheelchair. She'll never walk again, and I can't take it back. I've destroyed her life and mine."

Finally, William, who had been quiet until now, looked up, his eyes hollow. "I was homeless for years, lost and desperate. One night, I drove drunk and hit a pregnant woman." He paused, his hands shaking. "She and the baby survived… at first. But a few years later, they passed. My mind hasn't been the same since."

The Man in the White Hat nodded, his face impassive as he listened to each confession.

"You each have lived with darkness, choices that you can never take back. But tonight, you will each face a test. Redemption or ruin—it's up to you to decide which path you'll take. This test will force you to confront the worst parts of yourselves, to face what you've tried to hide or forget.

There are no guarantees, only choices. Only truth."

The room dimmed again, and the seven sat in silence, feeling the weight of their pasts close in around them.

Chapter 3: The Doctor's House

The light flickered and dimmed, and once again the scene around them shifted. The bare, windowless room faded away, replaced by a grand house, spacious and pristine. High ceilings, polished floors, and elegant furniture filled the space, giving it a warmth and charm that felt almost welcoming—almost.

But there was an air of sorrow here, something lingering in the quiet rooms and empty hallways. The house felt haunted by memories, the echoes of lives that once filled it.

The Man in the White Hat appeared, his expression calm, his gaze unwavering. “Only one of you will stay here,” he announced, his voice echoing softly through the house. “The one who feels this place as if it’s part of them.”

Noah’s face went pale, his hands beginning to tremble as he recognized the house, his house. Memories flashed before him—the laughter of his children, the soft voice of his wife, the smell of dinners shared, the warmth of a family. But his mind twisted under the weight of a darker memory, of smoke filling the rooms, of fire spreading, of cries lost in the roar of flames. He staggered backward, clutching his face, sinking to his knees. “No… not here. Not again…”

The others watched, their faces a mixture of shock and sympathy as they saw Noah unravel before them. He was trapped by the pain, by the guilt that had haunted him since that tragic night. He was alone in a world of his own making, a world that now took shape before them in the silent, empty house.

The Man in the White Hat snapped his fingers, and, in an instant, everything shifted.

The six others found themselves back in the familiar, suffocating room with no windows and no doors. They stared around, disoriented, before realizing what had changed.

Alisa's eyes widened as she took in the room, counting the faces around her. "Noah... he's gone."

She moved to the wall, her frustration flaring as she punched it, her knuckles scraping against the cold surface. "He's just gone!" she cried, anger mingling with helplessness.

The others looked on, feeling the heaviness of Noah's absence, wondering if they, too, would be tested, forced to confront their own darkest memories alone. There was an eerie silence, a feeling that each of them was being drawn toward their own reckoning.

As they looked at one another, fear and determination mingling in their eyes, they understood that this was far from over. The Man in the White Hat was waiting, and each of them would soon have their turn.

Chapter 4: The Last Chance

Noah stood alone in the house, trembling as he looked around. "How is this house still standing?" he whispered, his voice barely a breath. It had burned to the ground… hadn't it? As he turned toward the kitchen, he heard a soft voice—a voice he thought he'd never hear again.

He stumbled forward, eyes wide as he saw his wife and two young boys standing there, just as he remembered them, full of life.

Tears filled his eyes. “How... how is this possible?” he stammered, his voice breaking. “How are you here?”

For a brief moment, their expressions were warm, welcoming. But as he stepped closer, their faces changed, twisting into cold, accusing stares.

His wife’s voice was harsh, cutting through the air like a knife. “You killed us, Noah. Why did you put your work before us? Why weren’t we enough for you?”

The boys echoed her words, their voices full of hurt. “You left us, Dad. You cared more about work than your own family.”

Noah’s heart shattered as their words echoed in his mind, each accusation like a fresh wound. He dropped to his knees, his hands clutching his face, unable to bear the guilt that surged through him. “I... I’m sorry,” he whispered, tears streaming down his face. "I was wrong. I should have been there. I should have protected you."

His wife's eyes narrowed, her face hard with grief and rage. She stepped back, grabbing a knife from the kitchen counter, her grip steady and unyielding. "If you love us, then prove it," she said coldly, holding the knife out to him. "End this pain. End the guilt. Cut your throat—for us."

Noah's hands shook as he reached for the knife. He brought it close, his heart pounding, the weight of all he'd lost pressing down on him. But something within him shifted. He could feel the truth, the finality of the choice before him.

Dropping the knife, he fell to his knees, his shoulders hunched, his voice breaking. "I'm sorry," he choked out, looking up at his wife and children, their faces softening as he spoke. "I love you. I know I've done so much wrong. I admit that. I just want to be right… to live better. I'm so sorry."

Suddenly, the room seemed to brighten, and the vision of his family faded, their faces becoming peaceful. The Man in the White Hat appeared, his expression unreadable but his tone firm.

"You get one more shot, Noah. One chance to live your life. Don't waste it. No more mistakes."

With a gasp, Noah opened his eyes to a sterile, white hospital ceiling. Machines beeped softly beside him, and a doctor stood nearby, checking his vitals. "Dr. Hayes," the doctor said gently. "You're awake. You've been in a coma for eight months."

Noah's eyes filled with tears of gratitude as he took in his surroundings, the reality sinking in. He was alive. This was his second chance.

Smiling, he whispered, “Thank you. My last chance.”

Chapter 5: Mother and Daughter

The days seemed to blur together, a feeling of timelessness settling over the group. They had been in the room so long that any sense of reality felt distant. And yet, as the silence thickened, they noticed something that sent a chill through them: Noah was gone.

They looked around in confusion, each silently counting the faces, realizing with a mixture of dread and disbelief that he had simply vanished without a trace. The group sat in stunned silence, absorbing the realization that one of them had been taken, that they were not safe here, and that they too could be next.

The dim lights flickered, and just as the weight of Noah's absence settled in, the walls began to shake, pulling their attention back to the room itself. Shadows danced, and a vision materialized before them, pulling them in like a dream made real.

In the vision, a woman appeared, her face bruised and her clothes marked by faint, light-blue bloodstains. She clutched a small baby tightly to her chest, her steps hurried and desperate. She approached a door, knocking softly before quickly fleeing into the night, leaving the child behind.

Mary watched, her body beginning to tremble, her eyes widening as she recognized the woman. Tears filled her eyes as the painful memories stirred within her, and her breath hitched in her throat.

The Man in the White Hat appeared, his gaze fixed on Mary. “This is Baby Alisa,” he said, his tone calm but unyielding. “And you, Mary—you are her mother. That night, you left her and ran, hoping you could leave your past behind. But instead, you turned to needles and hard drugs, running from guilt and pain. You are still running, Mary.”

Mary’s sobs grew louder as she shook her head, clinging to herself as the weight of his words sank in. “I... I thought I could escape. I thought I could forget,” she whispered, her voice breaking.

“There is no escape from our choices, Mary,” the Man in the White Hat replied. “You’ve allowed your pain to control you, keeping you trapped in regret. But now, you have a choice.”

The other group members watched in silent shock, their faces etched with sorrow and fear, each feeling the gravity of Mary's truth. She reached out as if she could touch the vision of her daughter, the need for forgiveness clear in her trembling hand.

The Man in the White Hat's voice softened slightly, though it remained resolute. "It's time to go, Mary. This time, you and Alisa will come with me."

Mary looked up, her face streaked with tears as she met his gaze, her hand still reaching for her daughter's image, her heart filled with sorrow and longing.

"You still have a chance, Mary," he continued. "A chance to make amends, to be the mother you couldn't be before. This is your opportunity for redemption."

With a gentle but firm touch, he placed his hand on her shoulder. In that instant, Mary and the vision of Baby Alisa faded away, leaving the remaining group alone once more in the heavy silence of the room.

They felt the emptiness left by Alisa's ,Mary's and Noah's absence, realizing how swiftly each of them could be called to face their pasts. They were all bound to this place for a reason, and now they knew that the Man in the White Hat was not done with them yet.

Chapter 6: Deepened

With a single snap of his fingers, the Man in the White Hat transported them again. Alisa blinked, disoriented, as she looked around, feeling an eerie familiarity with her surroundings. She realized they were standing in an old, run-down house that seemed haunted by memories. Mary, her mother, stood nearby, her face pale and tense, recognizing the place immediately.

“Alisa,” Mary whispered, her voice trembling, “this was… our home. The one I left you in.”

Alisa turned to her mother, anger and sorrow flashing in her eyes. She had been abandoned, treated like nothing, even by the people who should have cared the most. But she saw something more in Mary’s eyes—an ache, a guilt that had grown heavy over the years.

The sound of footsteps echoed down the hall. Alisa froze, recognizing the figure before her—a man with hard, unyielding eyes. Her heart raced as she remembered her stepfather, the man who had hurt her mother over and over again. She watched as Mary shrank back, but she, too, seemed unable to look away.

“Come here, Alisa,” the man said, his voice dripping with false affection. “You know I love you.”

He reached out, placing his hands on her face, a twisted smile on his lips. Alisa’s breath quickened, and her fingers brushed against a knife on the counter. She grabbed it, feeling the cold steel in her hand as she looked into his eyes, years of anger bubbling to the surface.

The man leaned closer, and just as she was about to strike, Mary lunged forward, grabbing the knife from Alisa’s hands. Without hesitation, Mary turned on the man, driving the blade into him again and again. Her eyes filled with determination, releasing years of pain and fury with each strike. With a final gasp, he vanished into thin air, leaving only silence.

The Man in the White Hat appeared, his gaze moving from Mary to Alisa. "Mary, you did well," he said, a trace of approval in his voice. "You confronted the shadows of your past to protect your daughter."

Alisa looked at her mother, stunned, as the Man in the White Hat turned to her. "Alisa, had you used that knife, you would have run out of chances. But your mother saved you a place in this world. She has offered you her redemption."

Alisa felt her mother's arms wrap around her, the warmth of her embrace breaking through the walls of resentment she'd built over the years. The pain had brought them here, but for the first time, it felt as if it might be behind them. In the presence of the Man in the White Hat, they understood that they had been given one final chance—not only to face the past but to find a way forward.

Chapter 7: The Talk Between Worlds

In the hospital, Mary's body lay motionless on a sterile white bed, monitors flashing with erratic rhythms. Nurses and doctors worked frantically around her, their voices urgent, but to Mary, they were only distant echoes, faint whispers in the darkness.

Her pulse had grown weaker with each passing second. The heart monitor let out a sharp, piercing tone—a flatline that filled the room. The doctor called for a defibrillator, trying desperately to pull her back.

But Mary was somewhere else, caught in a place beyond the walls of the hospital. Her consciousness drifted between life and death, suspended in a darkness that was cold and endless. She felt weightless, as though floating in a dream—or a memory. Flashes of her past came to her, moments she thought she'd buried long ago: the warmth of a child's embrace, a night filled with regret, promises whispered and broken.

In the other realm, Alisa lay still, her own body unmoving, lost in dreams that bound her tightly to this mysterious journey. The Man in the White Hat looked down at her, expression unreadable, as though he, too, were waiting for a decision only Mary could make.

For fourteen days in the real world, Mary's body lingered in a coma, clinging to life by a fragile thread. But on this day, at this precise moment, the connection began to weaken. In the shadowed realm, Mary could feel a pull, faint but insistent, urging her back to the world she had tried so hard to escape. She sensed Alisa somewhere close, even though they were separated by an invisible barrier.

As the doctor prepared to try again, Mary heard a voice. It was quiet, almost like a whisper carried on a breeze, but it was unmistakable—it was Alisa's.

"Come back, Mom," the voice pleaded softly, a fragile thread connecting them across the divide.

In that moment, something shifted within Mary, and a glimmer of light appeared in the darkness around her. Slowly, she reached out, her fingers brushing against that faint light, feeling its warmth, its promise. She wasn't ready to let go—not yet.

But the Man in the White Hat's expression softened slightly as he looked at Mary. "There are only a few minutes left," he said, his voice carrying a quiet finality. "It's almost time."

Mary nodded, her gaze fixed on Alisa, her daughter who had grown so much and survived so much. "Alisa," Mary began, her voice soft and filled with love, "you've become so strong, so beautiful. I want you to be better than I was. Be great. Live the life I couldn't give you."

Tears streamed down Alisa's face as she listened. "Mom, thank you," she said, her voice trembling. "Thank you for being here and showing me the love I didn't know I had. I'll never forget this, or you."

They held each other tightly, both of them crying, feeling the weight of forgiveness and healing in their final embrace. Slowly, as if carried by a gentle breeze, Mary began to fade, her form dissolving until only the faintest trace remained.

And as she faded in the shadowed realm, her pulse in the hospital finally ceased. Mary's heart flatlined, and this time, the medical team did not attempt to revive her. Her journey in the physical world had ended the exact moment her spirit passed on in the other realm.

Alisa's eyes fluttered, and the world around her shifted. She felt herself being pulled away, a voice calling to her from somewhere far off.

"Alisa, wake up! Alisa!"

Her eyes snapped open to find herself back in her own home. Buck, her boyfriend, stood over her, looking concerned. "You've been asleep all day," he said, frowning. "You sure you're not sick? You even left the front door open."

Alisa stared at him, feeling a surge of emotions—relief, gratitude, and a lingering sense of awe. She reached out, her hand shaking slightly. "It was… my last chance," she whispered to herself. "Thank you, Mom."

Buck raised an eyebrow, confused. "What? Alisa, are you okay?"

She smiled through her tears. "Yeah, Buck. I am now. More than ever."

And as she held onto that renewed sense of purpose, Alisa felt her mother's love as if it were woven into her very breath, a final gift from Mary—a reminder that she would always carry her mother's spirit within her.

Chapter 8: The Descent

The heavy door swung open, revealing only a yawning darkness beyond. The group hesitated, their breaths catching as they faced the void.

"Let's just go," William said, stepping forward with a confidence he didn't entirely feel.

"No way," Luaryn replied, holding back.

Joseph rolled his eyes. "Come on, Luaryn. This isn't the first creepy thing we've seen today, and it's definitely not the last."

Brittany nodded in agreement, her voice steady. "Yeah, let's get out of here."

Reluctantly, Luaryn followed, and they stepped into the darkness together. The moment they crossed the threshold, the ground seemed to give way beneath their feet. They tumbled downward, each one screaming as they plummeted, their cries swallowed by the shadows around them.

Then, just as suddenly as the fall began, it ended. With a rush of light, they found themselves on solid ground, surrounded by towering trees and the sound of birdsong. The air was thick with the earthy scent of a rainforest, and sunlight filtered through the lush canopy above, casting a warm glow.

The Man in the White Hat appeared beside them, his presence calm and unmoving. "Change of course," he announced, his voice carrying an air of finality. “You’ll be here until we’ve completed all the tests.”

William glanced around, disoriented but intrigued. “What time is it here?”

The Man in the White Hat’s gaze was distant. “Time doesn’t exist here,” he replied, before vanishing without a sound.

Luaryn looked around, her eyes wide with awe. This place was vibrant and alive—a stark contrast to the dark, suffocating room they’d left behind. She wandered to the edge of a crystal-clear pool, kneeling to touch the soft sand by the water’s edge. Blue water rippled before her, mirroring the sky above, and pine trees lined the edge, their branches swaying gently.

But as serene as it felt, a sense of unease crept over her. She closed her eyes, whispering to herself, “This isn’t the end. The beginning hasn’t even started for us.”

The others joined her by the water, each lost in their thoughts, feeling the weight of the unknown. The rainforest was beautiful, but they knew it was only the beginning of the trials that lay ahead.

Chapter 9: The Cabin

A thick layer of fog blanketed everything, rendering the landscape invisible to the naked eye. Voices drifted through the haze as the group moved forward, eventually finding themselves outside a small cabin with a modest side house. It wasn't large, but it looked just big enough to live in. The buildings stood close enough together to be seen as you drove up to them.

As the fog began to clear, William noted, "Looks like the fog is lifting. Maybe it's just a change of scenery."

"No," Luaryn responded, shaking her head. "This isn't just a change of scenery."

Joseph nodded in silent agreement, sensing the same unease.

While they stood there, Brittany fell into a stunned silence, her face pale. Suddenly, she whispered, "The cabin… it's my parents' cabin." Her words hung in the air, and everyone turned to stare at her.

Before anyone could respond, the man in the white hat appeared out of nowhere. "Brittany, it's your time," he said, snapping his fingers with a familiarity that sent chills through the group.

In an instant, they were back in the rainforest, the fog clearing within seconds. Silence fell over them as they sat together, waiting. No one spoke, each person lost in their own thoughts, looking inward.

As Brittany approached the cabin, her legs trembled, knowing this would be a test. Just as she was about to grab the door handle, it swung open. Her father appeared and pulled her into a tight embrace. "You should've come home sooner," he said warmly. Brittany looked at him, confused, as her mother stepped forward.

"Are you hungry?" her mother asked gently. "You know, before we had everything together, we struggled so much. Your dad was going from one job to the next, and most of the time he wasn't working. I was cleaning houses just to make ends meet. But we pushed through because of you, baby." Her father nodded, smiling.

Brittany's face crumpled, and she suddenly broke down, sobbing. "I love you both. I'm so sorry… I killed you. I left you both on the side, telling everyone you were sick. I lied, I cheated… I hurt the people who mean the most."

The room darkened, turning an eerie shade of red. Her parents' expressions changed, their faces filled with sadness and pain. "You killed us, Brittany. Now, take this needle and feel the pain we felt," they said, their voices heavy with sorrow.

With trembling hands, Brittany took the needle and pressed it into her arm, whispering, "I'm sorry."

The man in the white hat appeared once more. "You used your last chance," he said softly, “but you’ll be okay on the other side. Remember, your parents still love you.”

Chapter 10: Poisoned Love

Brittany lay unconscious in a hospital jail, her body barely hanging on after a brutal turn of events. She had poisoned everyone in that secluded house by slipping a deadly pill into their drinks, leaving their bodies motionless in bed. Days later, a friend—concerned by her lack of response—came to check on her. As he approached the house, a foul, suffocating odor filled the air, and crows were circling above, a dark omen of what he would find inside.

Panicked, he called the police, who arrived and carefully searched the scene. They found Brittany, unresponsive, lying next to those she'd left behind. She had been unconscious for nearly a week, her pale face hinting at an attempted suicide. No one knew if she would survive or if she would ever be able to explain what happened in that eerie cabin.

As Brittany began to stir, her eyes fluttered open to see a man in a white hat standing nearby. She managed to whisper two words: "Thank you." Then, her breath grew faint as she slipped further into darkness. Her heartbeat slowed, drifting toward a realm beyond the physical, as if her soul were walking a thin line between life and the shadowed realm of death. In a final, quiet moment, she flatlined, her body motionless while her spirit moved with a strange, otherworldly grace.

Chapter 11: The Tree of Light

In the heart of the rainforest, Joseph, Luaryn, and William wandered, mesmerized by the enormous tree before them. Its leaves were aglow, dotted with lights that seemed to twinkle in and out, casting an otherworldly shimmer across the dark canopy. Luaryn was the first to notice something odd: some lights would fade out completely, while others flickered, then reappeared as if taking their place.

Just then, the man in the white hat appeared, his figure emerging silently from the shadows. “You’re partially right,” he said, his voice calm but with a strange weight to it. “The lights on the tree represent those who have yet to pass on. When a light fades, it means another soul has moved on. And when one blinks back, it signals a new soul has taken its place.”

Before any of them could ask more, the ground began to tremble, and in an instant, they found themselves transported, as if pulled through space, landing in an empty park next to a massive supermarket. The place was deserted, quiet in a way that felt unnatural. William clutched his head, rubbing his temples as he tried to make sense of what was happening. “This one’s on me, you guys,” he muttered, feeling the weight of a strange decision coming.

Suddenly, the man with the white hat appeared again, towering over them with an intensity that made the air vibrate. His voice thundered like an avalanche, echoing through the silent park. “CHOOSE,” he commanded, his words sending a shiver down their spines. And with that, Joseph and Luaryn vanished , leaving William alone, standing in the empty park, facing a decision that seemed to shake the world itself.

Chapter 12: The Choice

As William walked past the park, memories hit him like a crash in slow motion. He had been drinking heavily that night—celebrating a promotion to Vice President at his law firm. Everyone congratulated him, showering him with gifts and more drinks than he could handle. William, now an older man, had been with the firm since he was 18, and everyone agreed he deserved this recognition.

Later that evening, William stumbled to his car, dragging one of his legs, his body weighed down by the alcohol. He barely made it to the car before he started vomiting, his mind a blur as he slumped into the driver's seat. Against his better judgment, he started the ignition. He drove off, his vision hazy, slipping in and out of consciousness.

Then came the accident.

A pregnant woman was crossing near a supermarket when William's car struck her, knocking her to the ground. She cried out, clutching her stomach in agony as she lay helpless by the side of the road. In his drunken state, William drove off, leaving the scene in a panic. The next day, he scrambled to hide any trace of his involvement, even changing the color of his car in a desperate attempt to cover his tracks.

But the news caught up with him. The pregnant woman had died from her injuries in the hospital. Her family went public, pleading for justice. William pushed the memory back, trying to bury it deep within him, but guilt weighed heavily on his mind.

Now, as he walked near the park, a loud crash brought him back to the present. Looking across the street, he saw a woman charging toward him, her face etched with rage. He recognized her—it was the sister of the woman he had killed. William's heart raced as he turned and ran, desperate to escape. But she caught up, striking him across the back of the head.

“You killed two innocent people!” she screamed. “You didn't even care enough to face my family. You just hid, like a coward. And you think you deserve mercy?”

In her hands, she held a large liquor jug, tilting it menacingly over his face. He gasped as he struggled for breath, the weight of his actions crashing down upon him. In that moment, William accepted his fate, whispering, “I deserve worse.”

As the jug pressed down, his vision faded, and he found himself in a different realm, wandering a desolate alley filled with homeless souls—lost, abandoned. In this place, he was utterly alone.

The Man in the White Hat appeared before him, gazing at him with a look of profound sadness. “You’ll be a solid light on the tree.”

“A life without love,” the man said, “is a passing of the same.”

As William passed away in the real world, the homeless people who had been close to him looked up at the sky.

Chapter 13: Tree Calling

Lauryn and Joseph noticed a blinding light emanating from behind a colossal tree. Its branches stretched far and wide, shimmering with an ethereal, bluish glow. Lauryn squinted, trying to understand. "What... is this?" she murmured.

Joseph, equally entranced, shielded his eyes. "It looks like... the sun?" he guessed, just as a powerful wind whipped through the clearing, pulling them closer to the Tree of Light. Their feet lifted off the ground, and they floated before it, face to face, as if about to share an intimate conversation with something beyond their comprehension.

Just then, the Man in the White Hat appeared, his calm demeanor a stark contrast to the awe surrounding them. “Moon and Star,” he said, smiling slightly. “It’s always good to see you two.”

Lauryn and Joseph exchanged a glance, bewildered. They both spoke at once. “What?”

Lauryn found her voice first. “Can you explain?”

The Man in the White Hat nodded. “You two have been doing this since before time was created—guided by the Tree of Light. You’re here to collect and save lost souls, traveling from realm to realm. You’ve done this for eons, even if you don’t remember each time.”

Before he could continue, the Tree itself began to pulsate, the bluish aura growing brighter and more vibrant until it felt like it was filling the air, wrapping around Lauryn and Joseph. They could feel it—not just as a light, but as a presence, a voice within them. It wasn't speaking with words, but with understanding, a deep sense of purpose.

The Man in the White Hat watched them. "What happened?" he asked, as if already sensing the transformation unfolding before him.

Lauryn's eyes widened in realization. She felt a surge of clarity and peace, as if the knowledge had been there all along, waiting to be unlocked. "I… I'm Star. I understand now… why I'm here."

Joseph, too, felt the truth settle over him. "And I am Moon," he affirmed, his voice steady. “We’ve fought lifetimes, trying to guide and protect those lost in darkness.”

Their bodies began to glow with the same bluish aura as the Tree, resonating with its spirit. They understood now: they were bound to the Tree, born from its essence, eternal guardians of the souls who wandered between worlds.

Joseph continued, his voice calm and certain. “Our mission has always been clear. We seek the souls who do not blink, the ones trapped in darkness, afraid or unable to see the light. Those are our targets. We guide them, but we are not alone. The spirit of the Tree has always been with us.”

The Tree’s glow deepened, wrapping them in its warmth, as if acknowledging their purpose. Lauryn and Joseph felt it too—the sense that they were both part of something timeless, their very beings woven into the fate of all the souls who wandered through these realms.

Together, they stood before the Tree, their purpose renewed, the weight of countless lifetimes lifting as they finally remembered the truth: they were Moon and Star, the keepers of light, the guides for the lost.

Chapter 14: Time of Moon and Star

“It’s time, Moon and Star,” the Man in the White Hat announced, his voice filled with both pride and purpose. “You two have done an incredible job. I’ve watched you firsthand across lifetimes, and your work has never gone unnoticed.”

Lauryn and Joseph felt a warmth radiate from his words, but before they could respond, the world around them began to fade. Everything shifted, the familiar surroundings dissolving into a bright, sterile room with soft lights and the muffled sounds of a hospital.

A doctor's voice echoed through the room. "Push… push! It looks like… twins!"

The mother on the hospital bed gasped, looking up in disbelief. "Twins? That's impossible!" she said, her voice laced with exhaustion. "I could have sworn there was only one."

The doctor smiled reassuringly as he gently delivered the first baby. "Well, here's the first," he said, holding up a tiny newborn. "Just breathe, don't push yet. Let's get the second one here safely."

Moments later, the doctor gently placed the second newborn beside the first. A boy and a girl, both perfect and peaceful.

“What would you like to name them?” the doctor asked, handing the babies to their mother.

The mother looked out the hospital window, captivated by the night sky. She stared for a moment, as if in a trance, and then turned back to her babies. “Moon and Star,” she said softly. “Those are their names.” Her eyes shone with love as she whispered, “They’re my light in the darkness.”

Just then, the Man in the White Hat appeared in the hospital room, unseen by the others but very real to the twins. He looked down at the newborns, a warm smile on his face, and nodded as if approving their journey into this new life.

“I’ll be back,” he whispered, his voice filled with quiet assurance. Then, with a final glance at Moon and Star, he disappeared, leaving only a gentle breeze in his wake.

Moon and Star, once guardians of lost souls, had returned to the world, born anew, ready to bring light and purpose to those around them—guided, as always, by the spirit of the Tree and the quiet watch of the Man in the White Hat.

Made in the USA
Columbia, SC
04 March 2025

54681177R00037